RAINY DAY DREAM

MICHAEL CHESWORTH

FARRAR, STRAUS AND GIROUX

NEW YORK

For B.C., J.F.,
and Sophie

Library of Congress catalog card number: 92-4688
Published simultaneously in Canada by HarperCollins*CanadaLtd*
Color separations by Imago Publishing Ltd.
Printed in the United States of America by Worzalla Publishing
Designed by Michael Chesworth
First edition, 1992

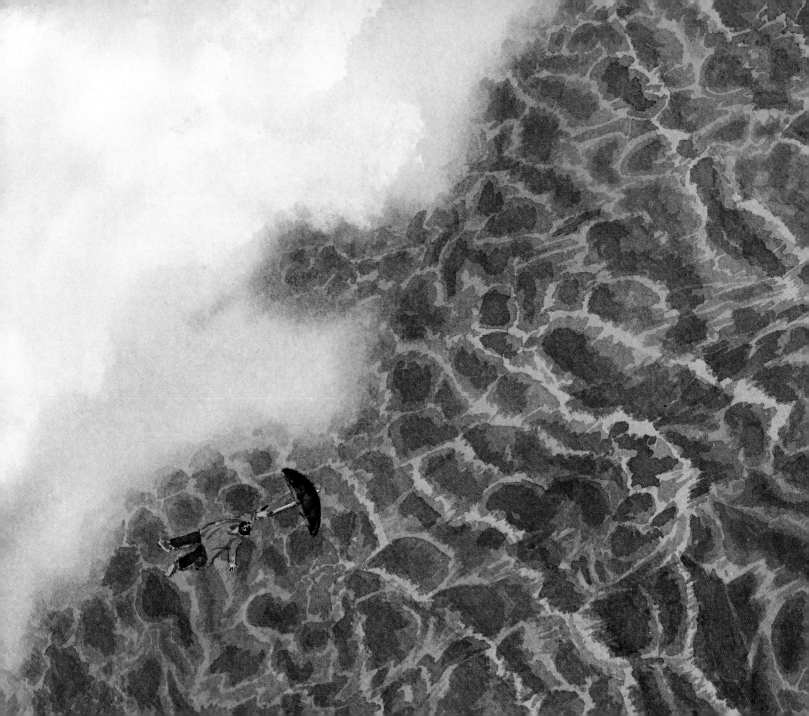

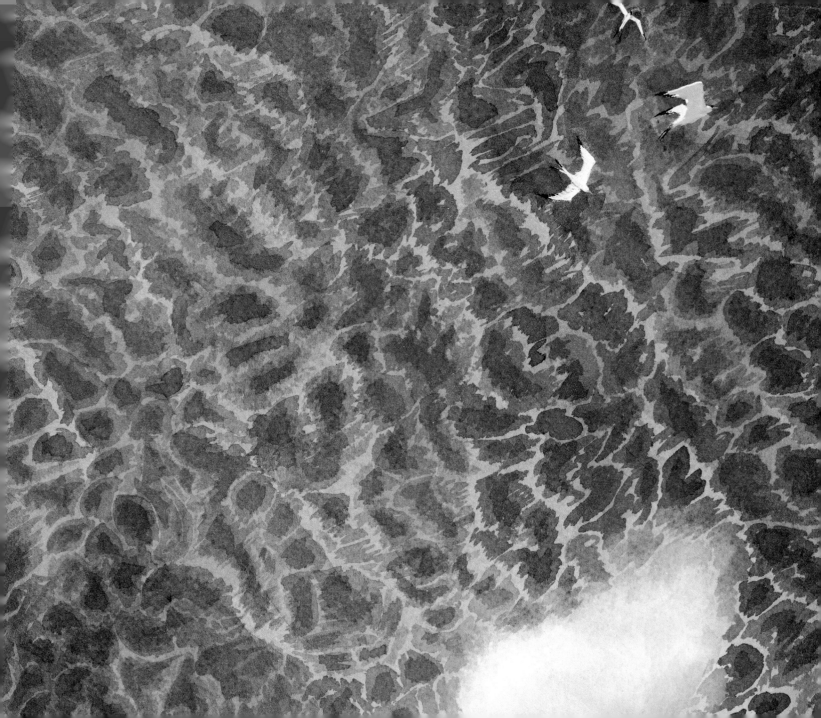